Puppy Princess

Super Sweet Dreams

Puppy Princess

Super Sweet Dreams

by Patty Furlington

Scholastic Inc.

With special thanks to Anne Marie Ryan

Text copyright © 2018 by Hothouse Fiction
Cover and interior art copyright © 2018 Scholastic Inc.

All rights reserved. Published by Scholastic Inc., *Publishers since 1920,* 557 Broadway, New York, NY 10012, by arrangement with Hothouse Fiction. Series created by Hothouse Fiction. SCHOLASTIC and associated logos are trademarks and/or registered trademarks of Scholastic Inc. PUPPY PRINCESS is a trademark of Hothouse Fiction.

The publisher does not have any control over and does not assume any responsibility for author or third-party websites or their content.

This book is a work of fiction. Names, characters, places, and incidents are either the product of the author's imagination or are used fictitiously, and any resemblance to actual persons, living or dead, business establishments, events, or locales is entirely coincidental.

ISBN 978-1-338-13430-8

10 9 8 7 6 5 4 3   18 19 20 21 22

Printed in the U.S.A. 40
First printing 2018

Book design by Baily Crawford

Table of Contents

Petrovia Royal Family

Rosie

Queen Fifi

King Charles

Rocky & Rollo

Chapter 1

Treasure Hunt

"Come on, Cleo! Let's look in the throne room!" barked Princess Rosie. The small white puppy's curly tail wagged excitedly as she bounded into the throne room of Pawstone Palace.

A fluffy gray kitten skittered into the throne room after her. "Oh wow!" Cleo the kitten said, her blue eyes wide as she gazed around the room. "This place is amazing!"

Regal banners with purple paw prints hung from the ceiling. There were two golden thrones on a little platform, covered with a canopy of violet-colored silk. The thrones had feet shaped like paws and plush purple cushions. They belonged to Princess Rosie's parents, King Charles and Queen Fifi, who ruled over all the animals that lived in the kingdom of Petrovia.

Rosie shrugged. The throne room *was* beautiful, but she wasn't here to admire the view—she and Cleo had more important things to do. They were on a treasure hunt! Rosie's chocolate-brown eyes scanned the room, but she couldn't see any jewels.

A gray rabbit in a starched black apron

with white trim hopped into the throne room and started brushing the thrones with a feather duster. It was Priscilla, the palace's chief housekeeper.

"Oh no," Rosie groaned. "Let's get out of here!" She started running across the throne room.

"A puppy princess should ALWAYS walk. She should NEVER run!" the bunny called out.

"Yeah, yeah," Rosie woofed over her shoulder without slowing down.

Not long ago, the very fussy rabbit had been Rosie's lady-in-waiting. Priscilla was a stickler for rules and tidiness. She had never wanted to play and was always bossing

Rosie around. But all that had changed when Rosie had sneaked out of the palace! She'd dug a tunnel under the palace walls and had an amazing adventure. Best of all, she'd met Cleo, a kind and helpful kitten who loved playing just as much as Rosie did. After helping Rosie find her way home, Cleo had become her new lady-in-waiting. More important, she was Rosie's best friend, too!

"Where should we go now, Rosie?" Cleo asked.

"Hmm. Let's try the ballroom," Rosie suggested.

She and Cleo ran into a long room lined with gold-framed mirrors that made it look like it went on for miles and miles. Guinea pig maids were polishing the marble floor with dust cloths on their little feet.

"WHEE!" cried Rosie as she and Cleo slid across the slippery surface on their paws. The ballroom was very grand, with huge crystal chandeliers, but there weren't any jewels to be seen.

Next, they ran down a hallway and scampered into the palace's dining room. An elderly tortoise was carefully setting a long, gleaming wooden table.

"Can I help you, Princess Rosie?" asked the tortoise, polishing a silver fork before very, very slooooowly setting it down next to a plate.

At this rate the table won't be ready until dinner time tomorrow, thought Rosie. But of course she didn't say this to Theodore. The tortoise butler had served the royal family loyally for many years. He knew everything there was to know about the palace and its history.

"We're on a treasure hunt, Theodore," Rosie explained.

"Ah, there are many treasures in the dining room," Theodore drawled. "These spoons once belonged to King Baxter II, the silver serving platter dates from the reign of Queen Roxie the Ravenous, and the crystal glasses were a gift from the Duke of Dalmatia."

"Not that kind of treasure," Rosie said, shaking her head and making her curly ears flop from side to side. "We're looking for jewels!"

"Well then," the butler said. "You need to go to the treasury!"

Of course! thought Rosie. The treasury was where the kingdom's most precious jewels were stored.

"Thanks, Theodore," Rosie barked. She and Cleo jumped over the tortoise's shell and hurried to a staircase. A bulldog in a guard's uniform was standing at attention at the bottom of the staircase.

"Hi, George," Rosie called to the guard as he stiffly waved her and Cleo past.

They bounded up the stairs and into a small room filled with cabinets displaying precious gems. In the middle of the room stood a golden chest. Rosie lifted the lid and showed Cleo the sparkling collars and tiaras inside. Diamonds, rubies, and emeralds glittered in the sunlight.

"Oooh!" Cleo cried, her eyes shining, "Treasure!"

"Who goes there?" someone growled. Rosie's brother, Prince Rollo, jumped out from behind a cabinet. He was round and cuddly, just like his big sister, but he also had a black spot over one eye that made him look like a pirate.

Another white puppy leaped out after him. It was Rollo's twin brother, Prince Rocky. "We found the treasure first!" he cried. "It's ours!"

"Oh no!" squealed Rosie in mock fright. "Another gang of treasure hunters!"

Cleo giggled. "I guess we'll have to fight them for it!"

The two teams of treasure hunters tumbled and tussled in a tangle of paws and tails.

"Grrrr!" growled Rocky. "My name's Grizzlebone, and I'm going to eat you up!" He bared his teeth, pretending that he was trying to bite the girls.

"Oh no, you don't!" Rosie shrieked, grabbing a ruby-topped scepter in her paws.

She backed away from her brother, waving the scepter around like a weapon. *BUMP!* She crashed into something soft.

"Oops! Sorry, Dad," she said, turning around to see a plump, white Maltese with kind eyes.

"What in the name of Petrovia is going on in here?" King Charles asked, gazing around at the jewels strewn all over the floor.

"Um . . . we were having a treasure hunt," Rosie explained, her tail drooping between her hind legs. "We got a little carried away."

The king chuckled. "I loved having treasure hunts when I was a pup." He looked around. "Actually, I'm on one now. Have you seen my sapphire crown? I need to wear it to dinner this evening."

"Here it is, Your Majesty," Cleo meowed. She bounded across the room and retrieved the crown, which was studded with brilliant blue jewels. She placed it on the king's head.

"Thank you, Cleo dear," the king said, patting the kitten's head with his velvety paw. "Now, I suggest you all clean up this mess before the queen sees it. She'll be coming up here soon to choose a tiara to wear tonight." The king sniffed the air. "Something smells good. I think I'll check and see how the cook is doing with dinner. She might need me to taste something . . ." The king wandered out of the treasury, patting his stomach.

Giggling, Rocky and Rollo both put on crowns and strutted around the room, sticking out their bellies and pretending to be their dad.

Just then, Rosie heard a noise. She cocked her ears to listen. There were footsteps coming up the stairs!

"Quick!" Rosie told her brothers. "Mom's coming!"

"Uh-oh!" Prince Rocky said. "I'm out of here!"

"Me too!" Prince Rollo agreed. The two puppy princes dashed out of the room.

"Don't worry, Rosie," Cleo purred. "I'll help clean up."

Rosie and Cleo darted around, quickly gathering up the jeweled tiaras and collars and stuffing them back in the golden chest. They finished just in time!

An elegant white Maltese with a fluffy

pom-pom at the end of her tail stepped into the room. Cleo bowed to the queen. Unlike King Charles, Queen Fifi was very formal.

"Oh, hello, girls," the queen said. "I didn't expect to see you two in here."

"I was showing Cleo the royal jewels," Rosie said. It was true—sort of.

Queen Fifi opened the chest. "Hmm . . . which tiara should I wear for dinner? The silver-and-diamond one, or the gold-and-ruby?"

"I like the gold-and-ruby one, Your Majesty," Cleo said shyly. "It matches your collar."

"I agree," Queen Fifi said, smiling. "Rosie, your lady-in-waiting has excellent taste." She placed the tiara on her curly head and said, "This is one of my favorite tiaras. It was a birthday present from the king."

"Wow!" Cleo sighed. "What a beautiful birthday gift!"

Rosie suddenly realized something. She didn't know her best friend's birthday. "Cleo, when's your birthday? Mine's in July."

"Actually," Cleo said. "It's coming up soon—it's in two days."

Rosie gulped. She only had two days to think of a special birthday gift for Cleo. There was no time to lose!

Chapter 2

The Perfect Present

BONG! BONG! The chimes of a grandfather clock floated up the stairs. "It's nearly time for dinner," said Queen Fifi. "Which means it's time for Cleo to go home."

"Awwww!" moaned Rosie. "I wish she could stay!"

"Don't you think Cleo's family wants to see her, too?" the queen chided Rosie. Then, more gently, she added, "Why don't you walk her down to the palace gates?"

They all went downstairs, then Rosie and Cleo headed out into the palace's beautiful gardens. Lush green grass stretched from the palace to the fancy golden gates. There was a marble fountain decorated with carved animals, flower beds spilling over with colorful blossoms, and lots of sweetly scented rose bushes.

Rosie and Cleo dragged their paws as slowly as they could, so they could have more time together, but eventually they reached the gates.

"See you soon," Rosie said, hugging

her friend good-bye. "I wish you didn't have to go."

"Me too," Cleo said wistfully. "I'd love to spend the night at the palace."

As Rosie watched Cleo scamper down the path to the village where she lived with her family, she thought about Cleo's birthday. Cleo was such a good friend. Rosie wanted to do something really, really special for her birthday. But what?

Heading across the lawn, her brow furrowed, Rosie didn't notice the squirrel pushing a wheelbarrow until he spoke to her.

"Penny for your thoughts, Princess," the squirrel said.

"Hi, Hamish," Rosie said to the

bushy-tailed palace gardener. "I was just thinking about Cleo's birthday. It's two days away, and I haven't gotten her a present yet." Rosie flopped onto the grass and covered her eyes with her paws. Sometimes that helped her think.

Hamish set his wheelbarrow down next to her. "Well now," he said. "What sort of things does Miss Cleo like?"

Rosie took her paws off her eyes. "She likes pretty things," she told Hamish, remembering how Cleo had admired the queen's tiara.

"The garden is full of pretty things," Hamish said, sweeping his paw around to show her. "Why don't you pick Cleo a bouquet of flowers for her birthday? I'd be happy to help you."

"That's a really nice idea," Rosie said, wagging her tail. "Thanks, Hamish."

But for some reason, Rosie didn't feel satisfied. Yes, Cleo liked flowers. But was a bouquet special enough for her very special friend?

Rosie decided to go visit Petal, the palace cook. She always gave good advice. Rosie went through the back door, which led down to an enormous, underground kitchen. A plump guinea pig the color of butterscotch was wearing a chef's hat and presiding over lots of other cooks in aprons. Gleaming copper pots bubbled on the stove and delicious smells wafted from the oven.

The guinea pig in charge peered into one of the cooking pots and shouted, "Daisy, give that soup a stir!" She nodded her approval as the parakeet cook took a tray of golden-brown cookies out of the oven. They were shaped like bones. "Those look delicious," she told her. "Be sure His Majesty's steak is well done," she instructed a bunny cook frying a steak in a pan.

"Hello, Princess," the guinea pig in the chef's hat said, noticing Rosie. "Would you like a snack?"

"Hi, Petal," Rosie said. "I can see you're really busy getting dinner ready. I won't bother you."

"Nonsense," Petal said. "I always have

time for you, Rosie. Now tell me what's on your mind." She offered Rosie a cookie, still warm from the oven.

"Mmm," Rosie said, taking a bite. "This is yummy."

"Don't tell the queen I let you have one," Petal whispered, winking. "She won't thank me for spoiling your appetite!" Petal turned and started to chop up vegetables. "How's that kitten friend of yours?"

"That's what I wanted to talk to you

about, actually," Rosie said. "It's Cleo's birthday soon, and I'm not sure what to get her."

"I'll bake her a birthday cake!" Petal exclaimed. "Consider it done! Does she like chocolate? Or lemon? Or maybe a nice carrot cake—that's His Majesty's favorite!"

"Thanks, Petal!" Rosie said. *A friend as sweet as Cleo definitely deserves a tasty birthday cake,* she thought. Still, it didn't feel quite special enough for someone so important to her.

"Now you'd better hurry upstairs, Princess Rosie," Petal said, shooing her out of the kitchen. "We're almost ready to serve dinner."

Rosie raced upstairs to her bedroom and rooted around in all her drawers, searching for a tiara. One of Queen Fifi's rules was that everyone in the royal family had to wear a tiara at dinnertime.

"Dinner is now served in the dining room," Theodore's voice called up the stairs,

Lying on her stomach, Rosie peered under her bed. Something sparkly caught her eye. Aha! There it was! She reached out her paw and pulled the tiara toward her. She blew dust off the diamonds and placed it firmly on her head. Then she ran downstairs and joined her family in the dining room.

"Finally," Rocky grumbled. "I'm starving!"

"I bet she couldn't find her tiara again," Rollo said. His own crown sat at a very lopsided angle.

Rosie stuck her pink tongue out at her brothers. King Charles chuckled, then quickly coughed into his paw when he saw the disapproving look on the queen's face.

"Children, please don't behave like a pack of wild dogs. Princes and princesses must always have good table manners," Queen Fifi said.

Sighing, Rosie tasted her soup, being careful not to slurp.

"Don't you like your dinner, Rosie?" King Charles asked. He had already eaten up all of his soup!

"It's fine," Rosie said. "I'm just not that hungry."

Petal and the other cooks brought out

the main course. The sizzling steaks smelled wonderful, but Rosie was too busy thinking about Cleo's birthday to pay attention to her dinner. She still hadn't thought of the perfect present!

"Look what Rosie did!" Rocky said, laughing.

Rosie looked down at her plate and saw that her steak was drowning in a white puddle. Instead of pouring gravy on it, she'd poured the jug of milk.

She burst into tears.

"Don't cry, my dear," King Charles said. "The cook can bring you another steak."

"It's not that," Rosie sobbed. "I can't decide what to do for Cleo's birthday!"

"There, there!" Queen Fifi said, getting up and stroking Rosie's fur. "Dry your eyes. We'll help you think of a gift for Cleo."

Rosie sniffed and dabbed her eyes with her napkin.

"You could get her a nice, new bone," Rollo suggested.

"Kittens aren't really into chewing bones," Rosie said doubtfully.

"Maybe a ball to chase?" Rocky said.

"That sounds rather energetic," King Charles said. "Maybe you could get her a new cushion—something big and soft and perfect for napping." He let out a yawn.

Queen Fifi rolled her eyes. "Cleo is a very stylish kitten," she said. "I think she'd like something pretty to wear. Rosie could give her a nice, new collar."

"Thanks, everyone," Rosie said. "You've all been really helpful."

But later that evening, as Rosie lay in bed, snuggled under her pink satin bedspread, she couldn't fall sleep. Her friends and family had given her lots of good ideas. So why didn't any of them feel quite right? She sighed, wishing that Cleo was there with her now—she always made Rosie feel better.

That was it! Rosie sat up in bed, her tail wagging with excitement. She had the perfect idea for how to celebrate Cleo's birthday. They'd have a birthday sleepover!

Chapter 3

A Royal Visit

The next morning, Rosie woke up early and bounded out of bed. She couldn't wait to talk to her mom and dad. She slid down the banister.

"What's the hurry, Princess Rosie?" Theodore asked as she landed on her bottom.

"I've got to ask my parents something,"

Rosie said, wagging her tail. "It's important!"

She ran into the dining room, where her mom and dad were eating breakfast. Queen Fifi was nibbling a bone-shaped biscuit, while King Charles was gobbling from a plate piled high with crispy bacon and sizzling sausages.

"Good morning, Your Highness," said a guinea pig maid, bobbing her head politely toward Rosie. "What can I get you for breakfast?"

But Rosie was too excited to eat. "Mom! Dad!" she barked. "I've thought of the perfect way to celebrate Cleo's birthday."

They both looked at Rosie, their ears perked up.

"Can Cleo come for a birthday sleepover?"

The king and queen exchanged looks.

"Pretty please with extra bacon bits on top?" Rosie begged.

Queen Fifi put down her biscuit. "You're still a little young to have sleepovers, Rosie. I didn't have my first sleepover until I was much older than you are now."

"I'm VERY mature for my age!" Rosie said, quickly smoothing down her fur to try and look presentable. She *had* to convince them!

King Charles peered at Rosie over the top of the *Petrovia Gazette*. "Hmmm," he said, frowning. "I'm not sure. Sleepovers can be very noisy, and a king needs his sleep so he can rule his land well."

"We won't be noisy," Rosie said. "I promise!"

Queen Fifi daintily dabbed the corners of her mouth with her napkin. "I have a proposal," she said. "If you behave like a proper puppy princess at our royal visit to the Petrovia Museum today, Cleo can come for a sleepover."

Rosie yelped in excitement and her tail wagged so fast she accidentally knocked into a guinea pig maid.

Queen Fifi raised her paw. "But ONLY if your behavior is perfect. It's a very important occasion—a new statue of your father is being unveiled today!"

"It's a deal!" Rosie cried.

Rosie didn't complain when Queen Fifi sent her to have a bath. She didn't even let out one yelp of protest when the queen made her wear a heavy tiara on her head and tied a scratchy ribbon around her neck. Soon, the royal family was perfectly groomed and ready to visit the museum.

The royal driver, a Shetland pony named Chester, brought the carriage around to the front of the castle. It had big, shiny gold wheels and comfy velvet seats. A golden pawprint crest was stamped on the carriage's purple doors.

Theodore helped the king and queen into the carriage. Then Rosie and the princes jumped in after them.

"To the museum, please, Chester," the queen said.

"Sure thing, Ma'am," Chester neighed. He started trotting and, with a jolt, the carriage trundled down the palace's long drive. "Lovely weather we've been having," he said.

As Chester chatted with the king and queen, the princes soon started arguing.

"Hey! That's my side of the seat!" Rocky said, giving his brother a shove. "Stay on your own side."

Rollo pushed Rocky back, squishing Rosie. But Rosie didn't react. She sat calmly, ignoring her brothers and gazing out of the window.

The carriage went past Oak Tree Hollow, where squirrels lived in houses shaped like acorns. Rosie waved a paw to her squirrel friend, Charlie, who was scampering around looking for nuts. They went through Hamster Hamlet, where a crowd of hamsters lined the road to wave at the royal carriage.

"Hi, Elsie," Rosie called, catching a glimpse of her hamster friend.

Rosie heard Twitter Town before they reached the village of brightly colored birdhouses. The birds who lived there greeted the royal carriage by sweetly singing Petrovia's national anthem from the treetops.

"You sound great," Rosie shouted out to the birds as they traveled past.

Soon they arrived at the museum. It was a big white building with marble pillars.

An owl wearing glasses greeted them as they climbed out of the carriage. "Welcome, Your Majesties," he said, bowing. "It is a great honor to have you here today. My name is Mr. Tawny, and I will show you around the collection."

Rosie and her family followed Mr. Tawny into the museum. There was a vast room filled with paintings. Some showed beautiful scenes of Petrovia with green forests, charming villages, and meadows full of poppies. There were paintings of bowls of fruit and bouquets of flowers. Other paintings were portraits of important animals who had lived long ago.

Mr. Tawny stopped at each painting and told them about it.

"This picture was painted by Casper Shorthair, the talented cat artist. It shows Sir Dexter Staffordshire, the famous explorer . . ."

As Mr. Tawny droned on and on, Rosie fought hard to stifle a yawn.

"It's lovely," she said, trying to sound interested.

Queen Fifi smiled at her approvingly.

Rosie's brothers were not being so polite. Rocky and Rollo were whispering loudly to each other instead of paying attention to their guide.

Next, they came to a portrait of a huge, ferocious-looking dog wearing a crown and a spiked collar. His long yellow teeth were bared, there was foam around his mouth, and a crazy look gleamed in his eyes. In his paws, he held a long silver sword.

"Who's that?" Rosie asked, shivering.

"Ah," Mr. Tawny said. "That is King Grizzlebone III."

"He ruled Petrovia a long, long time ago," King Charles added.

Rocky and Rollo started play-fighting with each other. "Grrr! I'm King Grizzlebone III," Rocky said, pretending to bite Rollo.

Rosie wanted to join in, but she knew she had to behave or she wouldn't be allowed to have a sleepover. She ignored her brothers and tried to focus on what the owl was saying about the next painting, which showed a plate of juicy bones.

They came to a room filled with statues. There were bronze and marble sculptures of famous animals in all kinds of heroic poses. There was a bird with his wings spread wide, and a proud-looking cat showing her claws.

Rocky and Rollo started playing hide-and-seek. Rocky covered his eyes with his paws and started counting, "One . . . two . . . three."

Rollo hid behind a statue of two hamsters shaking paws.

Mr. Tawny led the royal family over to a statue that was draped in a white sheet.

"Found you!" Rocky cried, pouncing on his brother.

Queen Fifi glared at the princes.

"And here we have the newest addition to our collection. It is a statue of His Majesty, King Charles, by the famous rabbit artist Claude Lapin."

Now Rollo was counting. Rocky hid under the sheet covering the new statue. His tail was sticking out, so he pulled it in and sat down with the edge of the sheet tucked under his bottom.

"Your Majesty, would you be so kind as to unveil the statue?" Mr. Tawny asked.

"Of course," King Charles said.

The king took a corner of the sheet in his paw.

"Oh no!" Rosie cried as King Charles gave the sheet a tug. The sheet slid toward the king, pulling Rocky along. The prince bumped into the statue, setting it wobbling on its pedestal.

The sheet swept off the marble statue. It showed King Charles, one paw raised and his tail sticking up proudly—and it was rocking from side to side dangerously. It was going to fall on Mr. Tawny!

I've got to do something! Rosie thought. If

the heavy statue fell on the owl, he'd be badly hurt.

She leaped up and braced the statue with her paws. It tottered for a moment, then settled back onto its pedestal. Phew! Mr. Tawny was safe.

"That was a close call!" Rosie said, feeling very relieved.

"Thank you so much, Princess Rosie," twittered Mr. Tawny. "You saved me!"

"She's a chip off the old block," King Charles said proudly. "The kingdom will be in safe hands when it is Rosie's turn to rule."

Queen Fifi wiggled a paw at Rocky and Rollo. "You two have been very naughty," she scolded the princes.

The royal family said good-bye to Mr. Tawny, thanking him for the tour of the museum.

"Come back soon," the owl said, waving good-bye with his wing.

"Not if I can help it," Rocky muttered under his breath.

"How was your visit?" Chester asked as Rosie and her family climbed back into the royal carriage.

"Lovely," Queen Fifi said.

"Boring!" Rollo said, flopping onto the seat.

As the carriage drove away from the museum, Queen Fifi turned to Rosie. "You behaved beautifully today, Rosie. You were a perfect puppy princess." The queen smiled. "So you may have a sleepover with Cleo tonight."

Rosie stuck her head out of the carriage window and, with her curly ears blowing in the breeze, let out a very un-princessy howl of delight. "Woohoo!!!!"

Chapter 4

Sleepover Surprise

"Can we pick up Cleo on the way home?" Rosie asked her parents.

"I don't see why not," her mother said.

"Chester," King Charles called out to the driver. "Can you please make a quick detour to Catnip Corner?"

"It would be my pleasure, Your Majesty," the pony said. He turned left and trotted into the village where Cleo and her family lived. They came to a main street with a few shops, a cute café, and a playground. Chester stopped outside a pretty, pale blue cottage with window boxes full of fragrant herbs. Rosie caught sight of a familiar furry face peering out of an upstairs window, her pink nose pressed to the glass. It was Cleo!

Rosie and the queen got down from the carriage, and Rosie thumped her paw on Cleo's front door. A grown-up cat opened the door. She had fluffy gray fur, blue eyes, and a pink collar. Rosie knew it had to be Cleo's mother—she looked just like her friend!

"Oh my!" said Cleo's mom, curtsying when she caught sight of Rosie and the queen. "What an honor!"

"The pleasure is ours," Queen Fifi said graciously. "Rosie would like to invite Cleo for a birthday sleepover at the palace this evening."

Cleo came racing down the stairs so fast she rolled down the last few, arriving like a fluffy tumbleweed at the front door.

"Can I? Please!" she begged her mother, scrambling back to her feet.

"Of course," Cleo's mother said, still in awe of the elegant queen.

"Yippee!" cried Cleo and Rosie together.

Cleo nuzzled noses with her mother to say good-bye, and then climbed into the royal carriage with Rosie.

"I've never had a sleepover before," Cleo babbled excitedly.

"Me neither," Rosie said. "But don't worry. I've got everything planned. It's going to be purr-fect!"

"Be a good girl!" Cleo's mom called after them as Chester trotted off.

"Don't worry," Queen Fifi called back. "She always is!"

Soon, the carriage was rolling up the long drive of Pawstone Palace. Chester came to a stop in front of the entrance and tossed his mane.

"Home sweet home," said King Charles. He sniffed the air. "If I'm not mistaken,

Petal has made stew for dinner tonight," he said, licking his chops.

After everyone had eaten dinner, Rocky and Rollo ran off to play tag in the garden.

"Do you want to play outside, too?" Cleo asked.

"I've got a better idea," Rosie said. "We're going to have a pampering session."

"Ooh!" Cleo purred. "That sounds fun!"

They hurried up a sweeping staircase to a bathroom with a white marble bathtub and gleaming gold taps.

"You want to take a bath?" Cleo asked, sounding confused. Rosie normally hated getting clean!

"No, silly," Rosie said. "I'm going to pamper you." She opened a cupboard under the sink and searched around in it with her paws.

"Aha!" Rosie said, finally finding what she was looking for. She pulled out her mother's grooming case. Inside there was a silver brush for styling fur, nail clippers, and several bottles of perfume.

Rosie took the lid off one of the bottles and gave it a sniff. "Pee-yew!" she said, wrinkling her nose.

"What are those?" Cleo asked, pointing her paw at strange-looking silver tongs.

"Maybe they're for curling your whiskers?" Rosie guessed.

She opened another compartment in the grooming case and revealed a rainbow-colored array of nail polishes.

"Ooh! Pretty!" Cleo said, her blue eyes lighting up. "'Pooch Polish,'" she read, examining the label on one of the bottles.

"I'm sure it's fine for cat nails, too," Rosie said. "Now what color do you want?"

Cleo took forever deciding. She couldn't make up her mind about whether she wanted cotton candy pink, ruby red, a sparkly turquoise, or a minty green.

"They're all so nice," Cleo said, sighing.

"Why don't I use ALL of the colors!" Rosie suggested.

Cleo loved that idea, so Rosie got to work

painting the nails on all four of Cleo's paws. She tried to be as careful as she could, but it was really hard to be neat! She did one nail pink, the next nail red, and the one after that blue.

"Oh dear," Rosie said, brushing on a coat of green polish. "This is trickier than I thought it would be." Polish dripped over the edges of Cleo's nails onto her gray fur. "Don't worry," Rosie reassured Cleo. "I'll clean it all up when I'm done."

Finished with Cleo's front paws, Rosie started on Cleo's hind paws. She accidentally knocked over a bottle of bright blue nail polish, and it spilled on the bathroom floor.

"Oops!" Rosie said, mopping up the blue puddle with a towel.

At last, she had finished painting all of Cleo's nails. "Ta da!" she cried. "You've got rainbow nails!"

But when she stepped back to admire her work, Rosie's heart sank. Cleo's nails were all different colors. But so was her gray fur! So was the floor, which was splattered with drops of Pooch Polish. And so were the fluffy white towels that Rosie had used to clean up her spills. Cleo—and the bathroom—were a mess!

"Oh no!" Rosie wailed. "This is a disaster!"

She tried to wash off the polish, but it had dried. It wouldn't come off!

"Mom's going to be so annoyed," Rosie said, scrubbing desperately at the spills.

"It's okay," Cleo said calmly. "I know exactly what we need."

Cleo rooted around in the cupboard and found a bottle of nail polish remover. "This will take it off," Cleo told Rosie.

They put the liquid onto cotton balls and rubbed off all the multicolored drips and smudges of nail polish.

"Phew! It's coming off!" Rosie said, breathing a sigh of relief.

Once they had got rid of all the spills, Rosie and Cleo cleaned up the marble floor. They put facecloths on their paws and skated around, like they'd seen the guinea pig maids doing.

"Whee!" cried Rosie, sliding across the floor. She grabbed Cleo around the middle, and the two of them twirled around and around on the slippery tiles. When the bathroom was spick-and-span, Rosie and Cleo collapsed on the floor, panting.

Cleo held out her front paws. "I really like my rainbow nails, Rosie," she said. They looked really nice now that they had been cleaned up.

"Good," Rosie said. "But pampering is hard work. I need a snack!"

Rosie and Cleo ran past the princes on their way to the kitchen.

"Cool nails," Rocky called.

Petal and the other cooks had finished

for the day, so Rosie and Cleo had the kitchen to themselves. The cookie jar was filled with home-baked treats. The fruit bowl was piled high with ripe apples and juicy grapes. The fridge bulged with tasty leftovers from dinner. But Rosie didn't want any of that.

She flung open the door of an enormous freezer. "We're going to have ice cream sundaes!" she announced.

"Want me to help you make them?" Cleo offered.

"No, no," said Rosie, waving her away. "You're my guest and it's your birthday tomorrow. I want to look after you."

Rosie took out two bowls from a cupboard and set them on a wooden counter.

She scooped a huge mound of chocolate ice cream into her bowl, and a pile of vanilla ice cream in Cleo's.

"Mmm!" Cleo purred, licking her lips. "My favorite flavor."

"We need LOTS of sauce," Rosie declared. She poured sticky butterscotch sauce onto her sundae, and sweet strawberry sauce onto Cleo's.

"That looks so good!" Cleo meowed.

"And now for the finishing touches," Rosie said. She added clouds of whipped cream to both sundaes, then topped them with chopped nuts and rainbow-colored sprinkles.

"Getting there . . ." she said. Rosie

popped a shiny red cherry on top of each sundae. "All done!" she cried. "Dig in!"

"Yum!" Cleo sighed happily, taking a bite of her sundae. "This is delicious, Rosie!"

Rosie's mouth was too full of chocolate and butterscotch to reply. She and Cleo gobbled up their sweet, gooey sundaes.

When Rosie had scooped up the last mouthful of melted ice cream from the bottom of her bowl, she wiped her whiskers with her paw and breathed a contented sigh. Then she looked around and saw the kitchen . . .

There were puddles of melted ice cream on the counter. Sticky butterscotch and strawberry sauces were smeared on the cupboards. The floor was covered with a confetti of chopped nuts and sprinkles.

"Oh no!" Rosie cried. "I've made a mess again! I've got to get the kitchen cleaned up or Petal will be really upset."

She hurried over to the broom closet but Cleo said, "Hey, Rosie. I've got a better idea."

Rosie laughed when she saw what her friend had in mind. Then she and Cleo lapped up all the drips and spills with their tongues. *Slurp! Slurp! Slurp!* In no time at all, the mess was gone and the kitchen was sparkling.

"This is the best way to clean up ever," Rosie barked. She felt like her stomach was going to pop!

Queen Fifi wandered into the kitchen

looking for them. "There you are," said the queen. "Have you two been having fun?"

"Yes, Ma'am," Cleo said.

"We made ice cream sundaes," Rosie said.

"Yes, I can see that," the queen said. She licked her paw and rubbed a smudge of chocolate off Rosie's nose. "It's time to go upstairs and get ready for bed," Queen Fifi said. "And be sure to wash your faces."

"Awwww!" Rosie whined. "But it's still early."

"It's past your bedtime. A puppy princess—and her lady-in-waiting—need their beauty sleep," the queen said firmly.

Chapter 5

Truth or Dare

After Queen Fifi kissed them good-night, Rosie and Cleo scampered up the stairs to Rosie's bedroom.

Cleo daintily cleaned her face with her paws and tongue. She lifted up the pink satin bedspread and started to climb into Rosie's enormous bed. "Good night, Rosie."

"What are you doing?" Rosie asked. "Just

because it's time for bed doesn't mean it's time to go to sleep!"

Rosie pulled out a stack of magazines from her bedside table. Cleo helped herself to a copy of *Furry Fashions* and flicked through all the latest looks. "Ooh! I love this," she said, showing Rosie a picture of a collar studded with pearls.

"Hmm . . ." Rosie said, doing the crossword in *Royalty Review.* She chewed on her pencil. "A five-letter word for something a princess should never leave home without." She nudged Cleo. "Can you help me? It begins with a *T.*"

"Tiara!" Cleo said.

"Thanks!" Rosie said, writing the letters in the squares.

"Let's play a game," Rosie said, tossing her magazine aside when she'd finished the puzzle. She opened her huge toy chest, which was carved with crowns and paw prints, and looked for something to play. "How about Pup-cheesi?" she suggested, taking out a board game in a box.

Cleo set out the pieces, and the girls began to play.

"Seven!" Rosie said, rolling the dice and moving her playing piece seven spaces. She handed the dice to Cleo. "Your turn!"

Just then, Rosie's bedroom door opened, and the two puppy princes came in.

"What's going on in here?" Rollo asked.

"We're playing Pup-cheesi," Rosie said.

"You can play, too, if you promise not to cheat."

Rocky shook his head. "Pup-cheesi is boring," he said. "Let's play something exciting."

"Like what?" Cleo asked.

Rocky and Rollo exchanged mischievous looks. "Like TRUTH OR DARE!" Rollo said, his tail wagging in excitement.

"How do you play that?" Cleo asked.

Rocky jumped onto Rosie's bed, knocking over the board game. "Well, when it's your turn you can pick truth or dare," he explained. "If you pick truth, the others get to ask you a question and you have to tell the truth. If you pick dare, you have to do what the others dare you to do."

"What if you don't want to?" Cleo asked, her eyes wide.

"Then we get to decide your penalty!" Rollo said gleefully.

"What do you think?" Rosie asked Cleo.

Cleo nodded. "It sounds fun."

"Who's going first?" Rosie asked.

"I will," Rollo said. "I pick truth."

Cleo thought for a moment. "Umm . . . what's your favorite pizza topping?"

"No, no, no!" Rocky cried. "Don't ask him that! Ask him something interesting."

"Ooh! I know," Rosie said, wagging her

tail in excitement. "What's the naughtiest thing you've ever done?"

"Hmm," Rollo said, his brow wrinkling. "That's hard. There's a lot of things to choose from!" He scratched his head with his paw. "I know!" he said at last. "I put slugs under Priscilla's pillow once."

"Oh, Rollo!" Cleo gasped. "That's terrible!"

"Yeah, well, she deserved it," Rollo grumbled. "She yelled at me for getting muddy paw prints on the carpet."

That sounds just like her, thought Rosie, thanking her lucky stars that the fussy bunny was no longer her lady-in-waiting. Priscilla certainly wouldn't approve of princesses playing fun games like Truth or Dare!

Rollo looked around. "Who's next?"

"I'll go," Cleo said bravely. "I pick truth, too."

"Let's see . . ." Rollo said. "What's the most embarrassing thing that ever happened to you?"

Cleo thought for a minute and then shook her head. "No," she said. "I can't tell you—it's too embarrassing."

"You've *got* to tell us," Rocky said. "Otherwise we'll make you do something— like poking one of the guards in the stomach."

"Well, okay then," Cleo said reluctantly. "Once at school I accidentally coughed up a hairball onto the teacher's desk."

"EEEEWWWWW!" cried Rosie and her brothers.

Cleo covered her face with her paws. "I TOLD you it was embarrassing!"

It was Rocky's turn next. "I want a dare," he said.

"I dare you to sneak into the kitchen and get us a snack," Cleo said.

"No! I've got a better one!" Rosie cried. "Open the window and sing Petrovia's national anthem at the top of your lungs."

"Here goes," Rocky said. He opened the window and stuck his head out.

"Hail to the land where animals are freeeeeeeee," he howled. "Furry and feathered, together in perfect harmonyyyyyy!"

The others rolled on the floor laughing as Rocky yowled the rest of the song. When he finished, he shut the window looking very pleased with himself. "You're the only one who hasn't had a turn yet, Rosie," Rocky

said. "What's it going to be? Let me guess—truth."

"No," she said, shaking her head. "I want a dare."

Rocky whispered into his brother's ear, a playful look on his face.

Rollo started giggling. "She'll never be brave enough to do that," Rollo said.

"Yes, I will!" Rosie cried, wagging her tail. "What is it?"

"Okay," Rocky said, narrowing his eyes. "We dare you to go up to the Haunted Tower."

Rosie gasped. She stared at her brothers, unable to believe her ears.

"See! I told you she wouldn't do it," Rollo said.

"What's the Haunted Tower?" Cleo whispered.

"It's the palace's north tower," Rocky explained. "And it's haunted by the ghost of King Grizzlebone III!"

Rosie shivered, remembering the portrait of the king she'd seen hanging in the museum.

"Who was he?" Cleo asked nervously.

"He was the meanest and scariest king ever to rule Petrovia," Rollo said, in a hushed voice. "His sword was always by his side, and he wasn't afraid to use it."

"He frothed at the mouth and tried to bite anyone who crossed his path," Rocky added with relish.

Rosie and Cleo grabbed each other's paws and held on tight.

"His ghost is said to haunt the north tower, where he died," said Rollo in a spooky voice.

"You can hear him howling and growling all night long," Rocky added. "That's why nobody ever goes up there!"

Cleo started to whimper. Rosie's stomach clenched in fear. Her brothers didn't really expect her to go up to the Haunted Tower—did they?

"What are you waiting for, Rosie?" Rollo asked. "Are you *scared*?"

"No!" Rosie said, even though her legs were wobbling. She slid off her bed and started moving toward her bedroom door.

"Don't go!" Cleo wailed, reaching out a paw to stop her. "It's too dangerous!"

"Don't worry, Cleo," Rosie said, trying to sound a lot braver than she felt. "It's just a silly story."

Just then, Rosie's bedroom door burst open. Everyone jumped. Queen Fifi stormed in with curlers in her fur. She did not look amused. "What is going on in here?" she demanded. "You should all be in bed!"

Rosie secretly breathed a sigh of relief. Now she wouldn't have to do the dare.

"Back to your bedrooms NOW!" the queen ordered the princes.

"Aw! I knew Rosie wouldn't do it," Rollo said, leaving the room as Cleo and Rosie climbed back into bed.

"Yeah. She's a scaredy-cat," Rocky called behind him.

Queen Fifi turned off the light. "Good night!" she told Rosie and Cleo, closing the bedroom door. "Sleep tight!"

Rosie lay in bed, but she couldn't fall asleep. Thoughts of King Grizzlebone III raced through her mind. She couldn't stop thinking of his picture, with its long, yellow teeth and razor-sharp sword. She shuddered and buried her head under her pillow, trying to block out thoughts of his foaming jaws.

Next to her, she could feel Cleo trembling.

"I can't sleep either," she told her friend, reaching for her paw.

They huddled together. Every time a floorboard creaked or the wind rattled the windows the girls trembled.

"Don't be scared, Cleo," Rosie said, trying to keep her voice steady. "The palace is really old, so it always makes strange noises at night."

CCCRRREAAAAKKK!

"What was that?" Cleo cried, diving under the covers.

"It's nothing," Rosie said. But this time she wasn't so sure. All of her fur stood on end.

She watched in horror as her bedroom door slowly opened. A ghostly white figure glowed faintly in the dark. The figure drifted into her bedroom and let out a terrible moan.

"*WHOOOOOOOOO!* I'm going to eat you up!" it growled in a low voice.

"AAAAAARRRRRGGGGGHHHHH!" Rosie screamed. "It's the ghost of King Grizzlebone III!"

Chapter 6

The Haunted Tower

As the ghost shuffled closer to the bed, it let out another spine-chilling howl. "I'm hungry for a puppy princess!" King Grizzlebone III's ghost wailed. "With a tasty little kitten for dessert!"

Rosie and Cleo clung together and screamed at the top of their lungs.

"Go away!" Rosie shouted.

"Please don't eat us!" Cleo begged.

And then the ghost did something very strange . . . it giggled.

"It's laughing at us!" Cleo whimpered.

Rosie recognized the ghost's giggle. She'd heard it many times before.

She hopped off her bed.

"Rosie, be careful!" Cleo cried in alarm.

"Don't worry," Rosie said. "I know how to handle this ghost."

She marched right up to it and tugged at it with her paws. A white sheet slid onto the floor, revealing the two princes.

"BOO!" Rollo said, giggling.

"We fooled you!" Rocky cried, who was rolling on the floor laughing. "You're such scaredy-cats!"

"Scaredy-cats! Scaredy-cats!" Rollo chanted.

"We are NOT scaredy-cats," Rosie said furiously. She grabbed a velvet cushion off her bed and pelted it at her brother.

"Pillow fight!" Rocky yelled, firing the pillow back at the girls.

Rosie hurled another pillow from the pile on her bed and bopped Rollo on the head with it. "Take that!" she shouted.

Whooping loudly, Rocky flung a lace-trimmed cushion at the girls. Cleo threw it right back at him with all her might.

Just then, the bedroom door flew open and—*POW!*—the pillow hit King Charles right in the nose.

"Oops! Sorry, Your Majesty," Cleo said.

"WHAT IN THE NAME OF PETROVIA IS GOING ON IN HERE!" King Charles demanded, rubbing his nose with his paw. Instead of wearing a crown, he was wearing a nightcap. And his usual jolly expression had been replaced by a frown.

"They were pretending to be a ghost!" Rosie said, pointing an accusing paw at her brothers.

King Charles sighed wearily. "Pups, you shouldn't be out of bed and you shouldn't have scared your sister and Cleo like that," he said.

"Tattletale," Rollo said, sticking out his tongue.

"They said they *weren't* scared," Rocky said, smirking.

The king held up a paw for silence. "You all need to be quiet and go back to bed," he said. "That is a royal order. If I have to tell you again, I will take away all your balls and chew toys for a whole week."

As the princes slunk out of the room, their tails between their legs, Rosie threw one last pillow at them. Then she and Cleo climbed back into bed. Rosie was fuming. *How DARE the princes call her a scaredy-cat!*

Rosie tossed and turned, but she couldn't fall asleep.

"What's wrong, Rosie?" Cleo whispered.

"I'm so annoyed we fell for Rocky and Rollo's trick," she said. "I'm not a wimp— but now they'll say I am."

"It doesn't matter," Cleo said soothingly. "I know you're brave."

"They'll never let me live this down," Rosie said. "I need to do something to prove to them that I'm not a scaredy-cat."

"Like what?" Cleo asked.

Rosie thought for a moment. What could she do that would wipe the smug grins off Rocky's and Rollo's faces? She needed to prove that she wasn't scared of anything— even King Grizzlebone III!

Then it came to her. She knew EXACTLY what she needed to do!

"I'm going up to the Haunted Tower," she announced, sitting up in bed.

"W-w-what?" Cleo stammered. "But it's *haunted!*"

"Exactly!" Rosie said. "If I go up there, the princes will never call me a scaredy-cat again."

"I'm not sure that's such a good idea, Rosie," Cleo said nervously. "What if the real ghost tries to eat you?"

"I won't get eaten," Rosie said. "Besides, ghosts don't even exist."

There was a long pause. "Well, if you're going," Cleo said slowly. "Then I'm going with you."

"Are you sure?" Rosie asked her.

"Of course," Cleo said, sounding determined. "You're my best friend, and best friends always stick together."

Rosie hugged her. "Thank you, Cleo. You never let me down."

Rosie and Cleo slipped out of bed and padded to the bedroom door. Opening it just a crack, Rosie peered out into the hallway. She looked left and then right. George, the bulldog guard, came marching down the hallway on his night rounds.

Rosie quickly shut the door. A moment later, she opened the door again and peeked out cautiously. George was nowhere in sight.

"Okay, the coast is clear," she whispered to Cleo.

They crept out of the room and into the hallway. Rosie steered Cleo past the loose floorboard that creaked when you stepped on it. They padded past Rocky's and Rollo's bedrooms, which were quiet. The king and queen's royal bedchamber was silent, too. The only sound Rosie could hear was her heart thumping. *BOOM! BOOM! BOOM!* It was beating so loudly that she was afraid it would wake her family up!

When they came to a corner, Rosie pressed her body against the wall, like a spy, and peered around the bend. She beckoned Cleo forward with her paw, and they headed down a hallway leading to the servants' quarters.

Moving stealthily, they crept past door after door. Suddenly, Rosie heard a growling sound. She froze. Was it a monster? Or worse—was it . . . Grizzlebones?!

"Listen!" she hissed, her ears twitching. "Do you hear that?"

"Yes," Cleo said in a trembling voice. "What is it?"

Rosie held her breath and listened. The low, rumbling noise was coming from behind one of the doors.

Zzzzzzzzzz, Zzzzzzzzzz, Zzzzzzzzzzzz . . .

"It's snoring!" Rosie said, relief flooding through her. "This is Theodore's room!" She stifled a giggle as she heard the elderly butler snort. She imagined him fast asleep, with

88

his head tucked inside his shell. "His shell must make his snores echo so they sound really loud."

"Phew!" Cleo sighed in relief.

They continued along the hallway.

"How much longer?" Cleo whispered anxiously.

"Almost there," Rosie whispered back.

Just then, a door flung open.

Rosie's heart seemed to stop beating for a moment. Then she grabbed Cleo's paw and pulled her behind a big potted plant. They peeped out from behind the branches and watched in fear as someone hopped out of the room.

It was Priscilla!

"Uh-oh!" Rosie moaned softly. "We're going to be in BIG trouble when she spots us." She knew that Priscilla would enjoy nothing more than reporting her to the king and queen for being out of bed.

Priscilla was wearing fluffy slippers on her paws and clutching a teddy bear. She was muttering to herself as she hopped very slowly down the hallway.

"The floor will sparkle..." she said dreamily. "The silverware will gleam..."

The bunny housekeeper stopped right in front of the girls. Priscilla was looking straight at Rosie, but she didn't seem to see the princess.

"I must dust the bookshelves..." Priscilla mumbled.

"Um, hello?" Rosie said. "Priscilla?"

But Priscilla didn't reply.

"I think she's sleep-hopping," Cleo whispered. "Let's get her back to her room."

They turned the bunny around and guided her back to her bedroom. She

continued to mutter about all the housekeeping chores she would do in the morning.

"Good night, Priscilla," said Rosie, tucking her into bed and shutting the bedroom door behind her.

"That was a close call!" Cleo said.

They hurried to the end of the hallway until they reached a heavy wooden door. Rosie looked at the door and shivered.

It was the entrance to the Haunted Tower!

Chapter 7

Grizzlebone's Ghost

"Why did we stop?" Cleo asked.

"We're here," Rosie said, trying to stop her voice from shaking. "This is the way up to the Haunted Tower."

She reached out a paw to open the door but hesitated. Even though she had told Cleo that ghosts didn't exist, she wasn't so sure. Lots of the palace servants claimed to have seen Grizzlebone's ghost through the tower window. Just last week, a maid swore she had heard mysterious thumps and bumps coming from the tower.

"You don't have to go up there," Cleo told Rosie. "Who cares what the princes say?"

Rosie shook her head. "No, I've got to do it," she said. "It's not just about what Rocky and Rollo think. I need to prove to myself that I'm not a scaredy-cat."

"Then I'm coming, too," Cleo said.

"Okay, here goes," Rosie said, gathering all of her courage. She pulled the heavy wooden door open. It creaked spookily and revealed a spiral staircase.

"I'll be right behind you," Cleo whispered.

Taking a deep breath to steady her nerves, Rosie headed up the twisting steps. Once the door had shut behind them, it was pitch-black in the stairway. Rosie couldn't even see the end of her damp, black nose—let alone the top of the tower!

"Hold on to my tail," she told Cleo. Feeling her way blindly in the dark, Rosie carefully climbed the stairs. With every step she took, her paws felt heavier and heavier. What—or who—would they find at the top?

Rosie wished with all her heart that she was back in her comfy bed. She paused for a moment, wondering if she should turn back. *You are not a scaredy-cat*, she told herself sternly.

Cleo started to hum quietly in the dark. Knowing that her best friend was with her made Rosie feel braver. *I can do this,* she thought. She climbed another step—and then another. Soon, she saw a glint of light shining ahead of her.

"Almost there, Cleo," she whispered.

When they reached the top of the stairs, Rosie gazed around at the tower. They were in a round room with thick stone walls. Moonlight streamed in through a few narrow windows, lighting up a room filled with old furniture and other odds and ends.

There was an old throne, its velvet seat cushion ripped and stuffing spilling out of it. A cracked mirror in a heavy gold frame was leaning against a wall. Near it was an antique grandfather clock missing its hands. A rusty rabbit-shaped suit of armor was covered in a thick layer of dust. There was even a chipped old bathtub full of knickknacks and a pile of mismatched plates and dishes. Dotted around the room were pieces of furniture draped in sheets to keep the dust off.

"It's just a storage room," Rosie said, laughing. "I don't see what all the fuss is about." The old furniture looked creepy in the dark, but it was harmless.

Rosie glanced over at Cleo, whose eyes were wide with fear. The kitten's tail was pointing straight up in the air, all of her fur sticking out as if she'd been electrified.

"What's wrong, Cleo?" Rosie asked.

Cleo pointed a shaking paw. Her stomach heavy with dread, Rosie turned to look. At the far end of the room, something was prowling!

A dog-shaped figure cast an enormous shadow against the wall. Rosie gasped as the ghostly shadow lifted its paw. It was holding a very long, very sharp-looking sword!

The painting of King Grizzlebone III flashed through Rosie's mind. The yellow teeth! The frothing mouth! The spiky collar! The long, sharp sword!

"It's the ghost of King Grizzlebone III!" Rosie whimpered. She and Cleo huddled together in fright, burying their heads in each other's fur.

The king's ghost was muttering to himself. "Oh yes, I'm going to eat you all up—every last bite." Rosie couldn't bear to look as she heard horrible gobbling noises coming from the ghost.

Rocky and Rollo had been right—the king's ghost haunted the tower and wanted to eat them up!

"We've got to hide," Rosie said. She spotted an old sofa with springs poking out of it. "Over there!" she whispered. Being careful not to make a sound, Rosie and Cleo crept behind the sofa.

From their hiding place, Rosie could hear the ghost smacking his lips.

"MMMmmmmmmm," the ghost said. It

sounded like his mouth was full already. Rosie shuddered. She was NOT going to let him eat anyone else.

"We need a plan," she whispered to Cleo.

"What can we do?" Cleo said under her breath.

Rosie thought hard. She put her paws on the back of the sofa and peeked out over the top. The ghost was rubbing its stomach. Then it wiped a paw across its muzzle. Rosie cringed, imagining the foam on Grizzlebone's jaws.

BUUUUUURRRRRRPPPP!

The ghost's belch echoed around the tower. Cleo let out a yelp of fright, and Rosie quickly put her paw across her friend's mouth to silence her. But it was too late—the ghost had heard them.

"Who goes there?" it called, swiveling around wildly. Rosie felt her blood run cold as the ghost started coming toward them!

Rosie looked around desperately for a weapon—anything would do. Grizzlebone's ghost was getting closer and closer. She had to stop him!

Moonlight glinted off the suit of armor, and an idea suddenly popped into Rosie's head. She crawled out of her hiding place and slunk toward the armor on her stomach. Rosie gave it a hard push with her front paws.

CRASH! The suit of armor fell onto the

floor with a loud clatter, right in front of the ghost.

"What the—" the ghost muttered, tripping on the armor and falling over.

Rosie ran back to the sofa and grabbed the seat cushion between her teeth. "Take the other end!" she shouted to Cleo.

Cleo bit the other side of the cushion.

"On my count," Rosie said. "One . . . two . . . THREE!"

They pounced on the ghost, covering him with the seat cushion so that he couldn't escape.

"Gotcha, Grizzlebone!" Rosie shouted. Underneath the cushion, the ghost wiggled around, trying to get free.

"Let me out!" the king's ghost barked. "That's a royal order!"

"No way! We're not going to let you eat us," Rosie cried. She sprawled on top of the cushion, paws wide, pinning the ghost down. "Go raise the alarm," she told Cleo.

"Got it!" Cleo said. She ran to the top of the staircase. "Help!" Cleo meowed at the top of her lungs. "Come up to the tower quick!"

Rosie joined in with her friend's cries. "We've caught him!" she barked as loudly as she could. "We've captured the ghost of King Grizzlebone III!"

Chapter 8

Midnight Feast

Rosie heard the sound of paws thundering up the tower staircase. The ghost squirmed underneath the cushion. "Come quick!" she barked, using all her strength to keep Grizzlebone from escaping.

George the palace guard burst into the room.

"Where is he, Princess?" the guard dog growled. "Let me at him!"

"Under the cushion!" Rosie panted.

Queen Fifi bounded into the tower room, followed by the princes.

"Grrrrrrrr," Rocky growled, nipping at the figure under the cushion. "How dare you try and eat my sister!"

Rollo pounced on the cushion, helping Rosie to pin the ghost down.

Grizzlebone let out a loud grunt. "Oooof!"

That's funny, Rosie thought. *I didn't think ghosts could feel anything.*

By now, more family and friends had reached the top of the tower. Priscilla was brandishing a feather duster, Hamish was waving a shovel, and Petal was holding a rolling pin like a weapon. Cleo and Rosie's yells had woken up everyone in the palace!

"Turn on the light, please, Priscilla," Queen Fifi ordered calmly. Rosie was amazed at how brave her mother was—she didn't sound even a little bit scared of the ghost!

Priscilla hopped over to the light switch and turned it on. Light flooded into the room, making Rosie blink.

"Now get off the cushion, children," the queen told Rosie and the princes.

Rosie and her brothers backed away from the ghost. Queen Fifi moved toward the cushion.

"Be careful, Ma'am," George said, blocking her way.

"Oh, don't worry," Queen Fifi said. "This ghost is harmless."

She lifted the cushion off the ghost. Everyone gasped. There *was* a king lying on the ground. But it wasn't mad, bad Grizzlebone III—it was King Charles!

"Hello, everyone," the king said sheepishly. He was clutching a cake knife in one of his paws.

"Dad?" Rosie said in astonishment. "What are you doing up here?"

The king got to his feet and brushed crumbs off his fur. "I was having a midnight snack," he explained.

Rosie still didn't understand. "But why didn't you just go to the kitchen?"

The king glanced at Queen Fifi, who had a knowing look on her face and was tapping her claws on the floor impatiently.

"Well, Queen Fifi doesn't approve of my sweet tooth," he admitted. "And nobody ever comes up here because they think it is haunted. I always keep one of Petal's extratasty carrot cakes up here. It's the perfect hiding place for my treats."

"I'm so sorry I thought you were King Grizzlebone III," Rosie said, throwing her paws around the king's waist. "Your shadow made you look really big, and I thought the knife was a sword."

"No harm done," said the king, hugging her back. "And it serves me right for being so greedy."

Just then, Theodore crawled into the room. "Here—I—am!" the butler cried.

"It's okay, old chap," King Charles said, patting the ancient tortoise's shell. "False alarm."

"I can't believe you actually came up here," Rocky said to Rosie, sounding impressed.

"Yeah," Rollo said admiringly. "You and Cleo aren't scaredy-cats at all. You weren't even afraid of King Grizzlebone."

"Poor King Grizzlebone," King Charles

said. "Your great-great-great-great-grandfather really doesn't deserve such a terrible reputation. His bark was much worse than his bite. He looked rather scary and had an unfortunate habit of drooling. But he never hurt a fly." He chuckled. "I think I've inherited his famous appetite."

BONG! BONG! The clock in the tower struck midnight. A new day had begun.

Rosie turned to Cleo. "Happy Birthday, Cleo!" she said.

"Yes, happy birthday, dear Cleo," the queen said. "As we are all wide awake now, we might as well have a midnight feast. What do you say?"

"Yay!" cheered Rosie, Cleo, Rocky, and Rollo.

They all trooped down the spiral staircase. This time, with all of her family and friends with her, Rosie didn't feel scared at all. The king and queen led everyone into the palace courtyard.

"Now, Petal," the queen said. "Why don't you serve the birthday cake you made for Cleo."

"Yes, Ma'am," the guinea pig cook said, bustling off into the pantry. She came out again holding a huge cake with three layers. It had thick white frosting and flowers made of blue icing the exact same shade as Cleo's eyes. On the top it read *Happy Birthday Cleo!* in swirly writing.

"Oh my!" Cleo purred, her paws flying to her mouth. "It's beautiful!"

"Princess Rosie said that you like strawberries, so I made a strawberry cake," the cook said.

Hamish ducked out of the kitchen for a moment. When he came back, the squirrel gardener was holding a huge bouquet of flowers. "These are for you, Cleo," he said, presenting her with the flowers. "Princess Rosie asked me to pick the prettiest roses in the garden for you."

"Thank you so much," Cleo exclaimed.

Rosie grinned to see how happy—and surprised—her friend looked.

"This is for you, Cleo," said Rocky and Rollo, handing her a gift.

Cleo unwrapped the package and found a shiny new ball inside. "I can't wait to play with it," she said, beaming.

Queen Fifi handed her a box tied up with a silky white bow. "This is from King Charles and me," she told Rosie.

"Thank you, Your Majesties," Cleo said. She opened the box and took out an elegant pink collar, studded with tiny diamonds. She gasped. "It's so gorgeous. I couldn't possibly—"

"Nonsense," Queen Fifi said, fastening

the new collar around Cleo's neck. "It looks perfect on you." She handed Cleo a knife and said, "Why don't you cut your cake now?"

Cleo cut slices of cake, and Rosie handed the plates around. As King Charles reached for a big piece, Queen Fifi pulled the plate away from him. "Only a sliver for you, Charles," she scolded him. "You've already had cake."

"Humph!" the king said, but he didn't dare protest.

The cake was delicious and everyone— except the king—had seconds. Soon, Rosie's belly was very full and her eyes felt heavy.

"Now it's high time everyone got back to

bed," Queen Fifi said, holding a paw delicately over her mouth to stifle a yawn.

After saying good night to everyone, Rosie and Cleo climbed up the stairs to Rosie's bedroom. As they snuggled back into bed, Rosie turned to Cleo. "I'm sorry nothing worked out the way I planned it to," she said. "I made a mess of your pedicure AND the ice cream sundaes. I'm sorry I took you up to the Haunted Tower. Your birthday sleepover was supposed to be special, but it turned out to be scary!"

"Are you kidding?" Cleo said. "It was so much fun! This has been the best birthday EVER—and it's only just started."

"Are you sure?" Rosie asked. "I mean, we

thought the ghost of Grizzlebone III was going to eat us."

Cleo hugged her. "Of course! Nothing is too scary if you're with your best friend."

Rosie smiled. "Happy Birthday, Cleo!"

"Sweet dreams, Rosie," Cleo purred.

Closing her eyes, Rosie smiled to herself as she drifted off to sleep. Her sleepover with Cleo had already been a dream come true!

Read on for more Puppy Princess fun!

Puppy Princess #3
Wish Upon a Star

That evening, Rosie ate dinner in the formal dining room with the rest of the royal family.

"Mmm, this stew is delicious," said Rosie's father, King Charles, licking his chops. The tubby white Maltese had already eaten two helpings.

Petal, the palace's guinea pig cook, *did* make very tasty stew. But Rosie didn't have much of an appetite tonight.

"You're very quiet, Rosie," said Queen Fifi, a perfectly groomed white Maltese wearing a diamond collar. "How was your dance lesson?"

"Awful," whimpered Rosie, hiding her face in her paw. "I stepped on Bruno's paw."

"You just need more practice," said King Charles kindly. "I'm sure you're not as bad as you think you are."

"Have you seen Rosie dance?" said Rocky.

"Her dancing's almost as good as her singing," said Rollo, giggling.

"I hate dance lessons," whined Rosie. "I wish I could quit!"

"No," her mother said firmly. "When you are queen of Petrovia you will attend lots of balls. It's important that you know how to dance."

"When I'm the queen, *I'll* get to make the rules," Rosie grumbled. "The first thing I'll do is ban ballroom dancing."

"We'll see," said Queen Fifi, sounding unconcerned.

"I've got some news that might cheer you up," said King Charles.

Rosie's ears perked up.

"It's time for the Royal Talent Show!" announced the king.

Rosie and her brothers yelped with excitement. Every winter there was a talent show in Petrovia, and it was always lots of fun!

King Charles hadn't finished. "Rosie," he said, "we think that you are ready to take on more responsibility."

Queen Fifi smiled at her daughter. "This year we'd like you to organize the talent show!"